Monster Mashers

More Devilish Fun with C.D. Bitesky, Howie Wolfner, Elisa and Frankie Stein, and Danny Keegan
From Avon Camelot

FIFTH GRADE MONSTERS SERIES
M IS FOR MONSTER
BORN TO HOWL
THE PET OF FRANKENSTEIN
THERE'S A BATWING IN MY LUNCHBOX
Z IS FOR ZOMBIE

Monster Mashers

Mel Gilden

Illustrated by John Pierard

A GLC BOOK

AN AVON CAMELOT BOOK

MONSTER MASHERS is an original publication of Avon Books. This work has never before appeared in book form.

AVON BOOKS
A division of
The Hearst Corporation
105 Madison Avenue
New York, New York 10016

Text and illustrations copyright © 1989 by General Licensing Company, Inc.
Published by arrangement with General Licensing Company, Inc.
Developed by Byron Preiss and Dan Weiss
Library of Congress Catalog Card Number: 88-92967
ISBN: 0-380-75785-0
RL: 5.6

First Avon Camelot Printing: July 1989

CAMELOT TRADEMARK REG. U.S. PAT. OFF. AND IN OTHER COUNTRIES, MARCA REGISTRADA, HECHO EN U.S.A.

Printed in the U.S.A.

OPM 10 9 8 7 6 5 4 3 2 1

Chapter One

That's Me!

Danny Keegan ran down the cement steps to the walkway that would take him to the Stitch in Time Tailoring Service. The sun was bright. The air was cool but pleasant. He was in the fifth grade and old enough not to be afraid.

But every time he walked down these steps a tiny twinge of fear bit him on the back of the neck. Did it matter that the shop was owned by the parents of his friend, C.D. Bitesky? Did it matter that C.D. and all his relatives were vampires? Danny was old enough to know better than to be afraid of vampires.

Vampires were no more frightening than werewolves or even kids put together on a slab the way Dr. Frankenstein used to put together monsters. He was positive of it. Yet, every time he came to this place there was that twinge.

A bell tinkled pleasantly when he opened the door and entered the big room that was the tailor shop. Because of the hundreds of shirts and pants and dresses and coats hanging behind the counter, it smelled cozy, like the closets in his grandparents' house. A tall man stood behind the counter speaking with a woman in a green coat and hat. He wore a gray apron over a formal white shirt tied at the neck with a black bow tie. A rank of needles with bits of colorful thread hanging off them was stuck through the apron.

"This will be done tomorrow," the man said, and took away a plaid shirt that had a rip in one sleeve. The woman said, "Thank you," and smiled as she passed Danny on her way out.

"Ah, Danny," Mr. Bitesky said, and bowed slightly.

"Hi, Mr. Bitesky." Danny bowed back. He never felt the need to bow to anybody but Mr. or Mrs. Bitesky.

"The others are waiting for you in our living quarters."

"Thanks, Mr. Bitesky."

Danny walked behind the counter, then down the hall, dark even in the middle of the day, where portraits of C.D.'s ancestors were hanging, each with its own little electric light. The paint on a few of the pictures was so old it had cracked in places. Even so, C.D. said they had to keep all the pictures up all the time. You never knew when a relative might drop in, and the Biteskys didn't want to offend anybody.

Even before he came to the kitchen, Danny heard laughter and a funny little voice crying "Papa loves Mambo! Papa loves Mambo!" Danny rounded the corner and saw a featherless rubber chicken chasing a boy around the room. The boy wore shorts and a striped shirt. His reddish hair grew down almost to a point above his flat nose, which looked as if he'd rubbed it in ashes. Danny knew it would always look that way. The boy leaped from chair to chair around the square table in

the center of the room while the rubber chicken leaped after him, madly flapping its naked wings.

"Get him, Mambo!" a tall girl shouted, and shrieked with laughter. She was dressed as any girl in the fifth grade might dress on a Saturday afternoon, but she had a knob on either side of her neck and a lightning bolt of gray in her dark hair.

Next to her was a boy even taller than she was. He had knobs on his neck, too, and a bird's nest of dark hair on his head. He only smiled, but Danny knew he was having a good time. Frankie Stein was a little shy, even around people he knew well. His sister, Elisa, shouted, "Get him, Mambo!"

To one side stood a very dignified boy wearing a white formal suit—what Danny knew C.D. called his summer-weight tuxedo. Two little fangs, barely noticeable, peeked from under his upper lip. A white cape with a red lining dropped from his shoulders. He folded his arms grandly across his chest and said, "Mambo will never catch Howie."

Not many people could catch Howie Wolfner, not even the bully of P.S. 13's fifth grade, Stevie Brickwald.

Near the big iron stove stood C.D's mother draped in flimsy white stuff. She covered her mouth, trying not to laugh at Mambo and Howie. Now and again an "Eep!" would squeeze out and she would turn around and furiously stir a pot on the stove.

"Hi, guys," Danny called.

Mambo forgot about Howie for a moment and ran over to peck gently at Danny's toes. "I wish he wouldn't say hello that way," Danny said. "It always tickles."

Elisa said, "Just be glad he is pecking with a *rubber* beak."

"I'm glad," Danny said, as he picked Mambo up and

4

carried him under one arm. Mambo had accidentally been brought to life by Mr. and Mrs. Bitesky. They'd been trying to cure the P.S. 13 fifth grade teacher, Ms. Cosgrove, of being a zombie. The ritual hadn't cured Ms. Cosgrove, but C.D. had acquired a pet.

Which was just as well. A lot of real animals were afraid of C.D. despite his gentle nature. Howie had the same problem, but he had a pet, too—Bruno, the mechanical dog that Baron Frankenstein had built centuries ago, and that Frankie had repaired just recently.

"Not on the table, Danny," Mrs. Bitesky said.

"Right." Danny put Mambo on the floor and said, "Ready to go?"

"Raring, my good man," Howie said. "Positively raring."

Howie led the way as the kids thundered through the dark hallway, stopped long enough to make a quick bow to Mr. Bitesky and to hear him say, "Children of Brooklyn, what noises they make," and chuckle softly. They bowed again and ran up the steps to the sidewalk.

Danny always enjoyed walking in C.D.'s neighborhood because it was so different from his own. Danny lived in a house with a front yard and a backyard. The house was not much older than Danny was. Almost any store he could walk to was even newer than that. His father said the stores had no character.

C.D.'s neighborhood seemingly had been there since dinosaurs ruled the earth. All the houses were made of ancient brick, though no two of them looked alike. As he walked by, Danny took his turn rubbing the face of a stone lion that was so worn it looked more like a sheep.

But that afternoon they didn't have any interest in houses or even stone lions. Their first stop was the Freezing Cow, where each of them but C.D. got a vanilla cone. As they walked down the street licking drips, C.D. pulled a thermos bottle from a pocket inside his cape and began to suck red stuff up through a straw.

Howie said, "Fluid of Life is no substitute for ice cream."

"Indeed," C.D. said. "It is a substitute for something more important than ice cream." He smiled, showing off his fangs.

"I don't want to know," Danny said, although he thought he'd guessed long ago what Fluid of Life substituted for.

They drifted around the funny little shops in C.D.'s neighborhood, stopping to look at whatever caught their interest.

There were a lot of antique stores that seemed to contain pieces of time itself: ancient clocks in the shape of people and animals, candle holders that twisted around like trees, brown pictures of sad-eyed people whose children were probably long dead of old age. A lot of it was just junk that nobody would ever want. Danny didn't even know what some of the wooden lumps and bent pieces of metal were.

The toy stores had no electronic toys, but even Frankie was delighted by clowns that fell down ladders, monkeys that climbed ropes, and propellers you could spin between your hands to make them fly high in the sky, no assembly required, no batteries needed.

There were bookstores with dusty tomes on high shelves, and record stores with men and women singing in foreign languages out of loudspeakers in front.

Even the empty storefronts could be interesting. Sometimes you could see strange bugs crawling around the show windows.

"Here's a video store," Howie said.

"Ah," said C.D., and solemnly studied the titles.

Danny said, "What does that one say?" The box showed a woman sitting calmly, up to her neck in a brick box.

C.D. said, "This is a popular favorite in Transylvania. It is called *Much Humor in a Cornfield After the Harvest.*"

"What's the matter with that woman?" Howie said.

"She is symbolic," C.D. said.

"It must hurt, being symbolic."

"It's a comedy?" Danny said.

"I never laughed," said C.D., "but my parents find it amusing."

"Not exactly the Marx Brothers."

"Who?"

While Danny and Howie tried to explain about Groucho and Chico and Harpo, they walked on. Suddenly Frankie called out "Wait."

Danny looked around and found they were in front of Cheapo City. "Wow," he said. "You can buy anything in here!" They didn't even have to discuss whether they should go inside. All of them were drawn in by the plaster busts of Julius Caesar and Beethoven, by the velvet paintings of bullfighters and Elvis Presley, by kitchen gadgets and toys and desk sets and other treasures unknown outside Cheapo City.

"I love this place," Danny said as he stood at the door looking around. "No matter how little money I have, I always feel rich when I come in here."

The group broke up, and Danny found himself walking up an aisle with Elisa Stein. She said, "Frankie is looking for little games for the Mad Room."

"You have every video game in the known universe down there, including some that Frankie invented himself.

What can they have at Cheapo City that's—Wait a minute. How about this?'' He held up a small game with a tin back and a clear plastic case. It was called Shootout! and the object of the game was to use a little spring-loaded stick to shoot tiny silver balls into depressions punched into drawings of cowboy bad guys. Each depression was worth so many points.

"That is the very thing,'' said Elisa. "Let us find Frankie and show him.'' They wandered through the store, not in any particular hurry. They stopped to look at a tray of small windup toys: cars that had people popping through the roofs and crawling hands and mobile sushi and creepy insects. "I really need this,'' Elisa said, and held up a Godzilla, no bigger than her thumb, that shot sparks when she ran it along the floor.

They found Frankie with Howie and C.D. looking through boxes in a section of the store marked by a big hand-lettered sign that said FASCINATE YOUR FRIENDS! CONFOUND YOUR ENEMIES! MAGIC TRICKS FOR ALL OCCASIONS!

"Look at this,'' Frankie said, "a carrot guillotine.''

"Off with their greens!'' Howie cried.

"It says it's guaranteed safe when used according to directions.''

C.D. held up a box and announced it was a disappearing egg.

"Very useful at breakfast,'' Elisa said. "Look at this, Frankie.'' Frankie agreed that the Shootout! game was exactly what they needed for the Mad Room.

When they'd all seen enough even Elisa had trouble getting Frankie away from the magic department. "Buy something,'' she said. "Here is a ring-on-string trick for thirty-five cents.''

Frankie shook his head sadly. "I will not. I have many tricks at home gathering dust.''

"You could put on a magic show for us," Howie said.

"No."

Frankie didn't say much, and changing his mind was next to impossible. They left the store with Elisa carrying the Godzilla and the Shootout! in a brown paper bag.

"What is next?" C.D. said, looking up and down the block.

On the other side of the street Danny saw a narrow shop with thick red stripes painted diagonally across the front. He grinned, remembering that place, and said, "There's Zelda Bella's Fruit. We could go say hello."

"Capital idea," Howie said, and led the way to the corner, where they waited for the light to change. There had been a time when Howie was tired of being a werewolf, and he thought that a Gypsy might be able to help change him into an average boy. The only Gypsy they'd been able to find had been Zelda Bella. She'd sold them a magic spell and some old fruit, but Howie had never found out if either of them were any good.

They crossed the street and ran to the door of Zelda Bella's Fruit. It would not open.

"Locked," Frankie said. He looked under his hand through the glass, and the others joined him. The shadowy inside of the store looked empty to Danny. All the old fruit had been cleaned out, which meant the flies were probably gone, too. Even the faded red curtain that separated the front of the store from the place where Zelda Bella lived in back was no longer there.

"Where could she be?" C.D. said.

"Here is the answer," Elisa said, and pointed to a sheet of paper posted next to the door. On it a thick arrow pointed to a photograph of Zelda Bella, and the hand-printed words THAT'S ME! Under that in professional

9

type it said, "Watch 'Mother Scary's Matinee' every Saturday afternoon!"

"Can this mean what it seems to mean?" Howie said.

Danny said excitedly, "Zelda Bella must be the new Mother Scary. I watch that show all the time!" He saw the disapproving looks on the faces of his friends. "Or rather I used to. For a while. Sometimes."

C.D. said, "Mother Scary is the host of a program that shows monster movies, is she not?"

"Well, yeah," Danny said.

Elisa said, "Monster movies have caused us much bother."

"Even so," said Howie, "she is somebody we know. I, for one, have never seen anybody I know on television."

"Perhaps," Frankie said, "watching once will not hurt us."

"We'd better hurry, then," Danny said as he looked at his watch. "The show starts in less than an hour."

Chapter Two

Some Like It Scary

What Danny said was undeniably true. Still he and the monster kids just stood there in front of Zelda Bella's Fruit. Howie spoke for them all when he said, "That's fine. But where will we do the deed?" He seemed worried.

"C.D.'s house is closest," Frankie said, but he did not seem happy about it.

The monster kids looked at the toes of their shoes as they shuffled them. Then Danny said, "Sheesh, it's just a TV show."

"Perhaps," said C.D. firmly, "but we do not watch monster movies at my house."

"Also not ours," said Elisa.

"Me, too," said Howie.

"Look," Danny said, "if you don't want to do this, that's OK."

"No, no," said Elisa. "This is not the Old Country. We must not be afraid or make judgments."

"Besides," said Howie, "Zelda Bella is our friend. We should support her by watching her show. I think."

11

"All right, then," Danny said. "Let's watch at my house."

"Bully," said Howie.

Frankie said, "Yes. But can we catch a bus in time?"

"You wait for the bus," C.D. said. "I will meet you there." He leaped into the air, and suddenly there was a bat hanging in his place. The bat flapped off in the direction of Danny's house.

"Why does it distress me so when he does that?" Howie said.

"I don't know," Danny said. "You should hear yourself howl when you're in wolf mode."

The bus seemed to take forever to come. But when it arrived at last, the ride to the Keegan house was short. They ran from the bus stop and met C.D. in front. He was sucking on his Fluid of Life and his face was a little red, but he said, "I am much refreshed and ready for the ordeal to come."

"Look," said Danny, "if you guys don't want to do this—"

Howie interrupted and said excitedly, "We want to do this. Please open the door."

"Uh," said Danny, "you guys wait out here for a minute. I'll put Harryhausen in the backyard."

"I'm home," Danny shouted as he entered the house. He found Harryhausen in the kitchen, asleep on the spot in front of the sink where Mrs. Keegan sometimes stood. As gently as he could, he picked the dog up and half carried, half dragged him out into the backyard. Barely awake, Harryhausen licked Danny's hand.

Danny ran back to the front door and let his friends into the house. He shouted, "Elisa and Howie and C.D. are with me," and slammed the door.

Somebody hit the deck upstairs, and a moment later

Danny's little sister, Barbara, was leaping down the stairs to hug Elisa. It was difficult for Danny to believe that Barbara had once been afraid of Elisa. Now they were Girls' Pathfinders together, and went on hikes and cookouts and did all kinds of other rustic things.

"What is that smell?" Howie said, wrinkling his nose in the air.

"It is Eau de Springtime," Barbara said, sniffing her hands. "I got it at Cheapo City."

Howie smiled and said, "It certainly is strong."

"I hope so," Barbara said. "I paid a whole dollar for it."

Danny said, "Come on if you're coming," and ran into the living room to switch on the television. His father was already there reading a book at one end of the couch. "What's going on?"

Breathlessly, Danny said, "We're going to watch 'Mother Scary's Matinee.'"

"Gee," Mr. Keegan said, "I haven't seen that since I was a kid." He closed his book on a finger, and Danny had the suspicion that his father had settled in for the duration of the program. Danny liked his parents, mostly, but they always did something embarrassing when his friends were around.

"Just some old monster movie," Danny said.

"I love old monster movies," Mr. Keegan said, and Danny knew there would be no way to get rid of him.

As the monster kids gathered around, the TV came to life. Words dripped down the TV screen while a guy with a scary voice said, "Welcome to 'Mother Scary's Matinee' and another movie guaranteed to keep you on the edge of your seat. *If* you can stay in your chair at all." A woman screamed horribly. Danny said "Oooo!"

13

and went over to sit next to his father. Barbara was clutching Elisa's arm.

Nobody else seemed impressed. His friends were all grim-faced and tight-lipped. Howie had his arms folded across his chest. Maybe watching this show hadn't been such a good idea, no matter who was on it.

On the TV, the camera seemed to dive through thick fog until it homed in on a large, solid woman wearing a tattered black sack and a tall, pointy hat that was bent at the top. She was stirring some gorpy-looking stuff with the handle of her twig broom and singing: "Double double toil and trouble, fire burn and cauldron bubble!"

She pulled a rubbery-looking bat from the cauldron, and it seemed to wiggle in her fingers. "How did that get in there?" she shrieked, and cackled as she threw it aside.

Danny studied Mother Scary. She had a long, crooked nose and a wart the size of a coat button on her cheek. A lot of black stuff was rubbed around her eyes, and her lips were blue. Still, there was no denying that, under all the makeup, Mother Scary was really Zelda Bella. Danny thought he even saw a gold ring dangling from one ear among the long, stringy hair.

"Wow," Danny said.

"It *is* Zelda Bella," Howie said softly. He didn't sound angry anymore.

"Have we got a movie for you today!" Mother Scary shrieked.

Barbara said, "If she keeps up that screaming, she'll ruin her throat."

Mother Scary hit a gong with a small hammer, and a guy dressed like a zombie staggered into the picture carrying a silver pot. He handed the pot to Mother

Scary, smiled like a goof to the camera, and stumbled off again.

"He is very silly," Elisa said, and laughed.

That's better, Danny thought. Maybe my friends won't hate me for suggesting this after all.

Mother Scary opened the pot and showed it around. "Why, there's nothing in here, you fool!" And indeed, there was not. "'I'll fix that.'" She gestured at the pot and a fireball exploded from inside. Quickly she put the top back on, then shook the pot as if she were a bartender mixing a drink.

She held up the pot on the upraised fingers of one hand and dramatically pulled off the top. Once more there seemed to be nothing inside. Crooning like a happy fire siren, Mother Scary reached in and lifted out a big frog carrying a folded newspaper in its mouth. For all Danny could tell, the frog could have been rubber, just like the bat. She took the newspaper and dumped the frog into the cauldron, making a big splash, then threw the pot over her shoulder. It landed with a crash that made her cringe.

"Her magic is a little old," C.D. said.

"Indeed," Frankie said. "I have many of these tricks at home."

Cackling, Mother Scary pulled on a string that went down inside the front of her dress. Hand over hand, she pulled and pulled and pulled and at last pulled out a scissors. After closely inspecting the newspaper, she snipped off one corner of it. As she quickly unfolded the newspaper, she said, "Today's movie is . . ." While she held the unfolded newspaper up to the camera, she said, *Some Like It Scary.* And, in fact, that's what the cutout parts of the unfolded newspaper said.

The picture went out of focus and a commercial for a breakfast cereal called Wonky Wheats began.

While cute animated insects danced in a cereal bowl, Mr. Keegan said, "She's not as good as the Mother Scary we had when *I* was a kid."

Howie said, "There was a Mother Scary way back then?"

"Not so long ago, really," Mr. Keegan said, seemingly a little miffed. "She was a little thinner and she wore a hat that looked like a black shower cap, but the best part was the patented Mother Scary Salute." He gazed upward, remembering.

"What was the salute like?" Barbara said. Elisa carefully uncurled Barbara's fingers from her arm and patted her hand.

"Let's see," Mr. Keegan said, "it went like this." He raised both hands in the air and shook them while he cried "Boo!" and then cackled like a witch.

Barbara made the salute back at him, and pretty soon everybody was waving hands in the air and crying "Boo!" and cackling. After a while they couldn't do it anymore because they were laughing so hard.

Danny said, "And Mom married you anyway."

"Amazing," Barbara said.

Mr. Keegan looked hurt and began to tickle Danny, causing Danny to convulse with laughter. The front door opened and Mrs. Keegan walked in. She was dressed in a crisp flower-print dress and had a matching purse slung over her shoulder. She stood at the entrance to the living room, a bewildered look on her face. "What's going on?" she said.

Barbara said, "Daddy's reliving his childhood."

"No I'm not," Mr. Keegan said as seriously as he

17

could manage. "We were just waiting for the monster movie to start."

"Monster movie?" Mrs. Keegan said as she looked around the living room. "Hi, kids. No, C.D., you don't have to get up and kiss my hand."

"Perhaps you would watch with us?" Elisa said.

"No way. I've been social all afternoon. Out with 'the girls,' you know. I'm going upstairs to take a long, hot bath." As she climbed the stairs, melodramatic organ music began and the words *Some Like It Scary* rippled into view on the TV screen.

The movie was about a half-bright scientist named Baron Volga who marched around all the time with his finger in the air, announcing things like "A genius such as myself is not bound by the rules of other men." Then he played with stuff that looked like old radio sets and milk bottles full of colored water. Danny didn't see how this particular monster movie could offend anybody. And indeed, his friends seemed to enjoy it as much as he and Barbara and their dad did.

"He is not properly grounded," Frankie said.

"That's for sure," Barbara said.

But it didn't seem to matter. The machines worked, spinning and throwing off big sparks.

"Look," said Howie, "the machine stuff is in black and white."

"Yes," said C.D., "and the rest of the movie is in color! Perhaps it is symbolic?"

"Yeah," said Barbara, "symbolic of stupidity."

It wasn't difficult to find things wrong with the movie. People would walk out of one room dressed in evening clothes and into the next dressed for tennis. The monster made by Baron Volga stumbled into things. The actor who played the monster obviously couldn't see where he was going.

"Look," said C.D., "is that the same vampire?"

"They call him Count Mort, just like the other guy, but . . ." Mr. Keegan peered at the TV. "No. My goodness. It's a different actor entirely." He laughed so hard that everybody else laughed too.

At one point, the werewolf was supposed to be eating the bones of his long-decayed wife. "Graham crackers," Howie said.

Danny could see Howie was right. They didn't look like bones at all. The people who made the movie hadn't even bothered to break off the square corners.

During a break, Mother Scary snapped and restored a matchstick and promised that the big finish was coming up. There was a run for the bathroom. Danny made it back just in time to see the cardboard model of Castle Volga—no more realistic than Ms. Cosgrove's model of P.S. 13—explode in a spout of sparks. Everybody cheered.

By the time the movie was over they were worn out from laughing. They'd seen the same Wonky Wheats commercial eight times (they'd counted), and the monster kids felt a lot better about monster movies.

"Surely no one could take this seriously," Howie said.

"Surely not," C.D. said.

Frankie nodded, and Elisa did the old Mother Scary Salute. This set them all off again.

"Here's Mother Scary again," Danny said.

"Doesn't she look capital?" Howie said.

Barbara put a finger to her lips.

Mother Scary was sitting on a stool next to her smoking cauldron. She said, "Did you enjoy that?" There were a lot of hisses and boos and catcalls from people in the studio with her. She cackled and said, "If you did, let me know. I'll send somebody right over with a straitjacket." She whooped and slapped her knees.

"And now a special announcement for all my little familiars out there. You can enter Mother Scary's 'Do-It-Yourself Monster Contest.' "

"Shush," said Barbara, though nobody had made a sound.

Mother Scary went on: "All you have to do is send me a photograph of yourself dressed as your favorite monster. The five best monsters will be my guests right here on 'Mother Scary's Matinee.' " She gave the address of the TV station. The camera came in very close on Mother Scary's face, and she said, "Enter if you dare," then shrieked and cackled and stood up and began to stir her cauldron again.

Her theme music came up and the credits rolled across the picture and the show was over. But nobody noticed. If they were like Danny, they were thinking about entering the contest and winning. After all, who could be better monsters than monsters themselves?

Chapter Three

One Picture Is Worth a Thousand Monsters

Danny and the others ran up the stairs, in their excitement perhaps making a little more noise than they had to. When everybody was in Danny's room, Danny shut the door and sat down on the bed. Barbara sat next to him. C.D. perched on Danny's desk chair, and Howie and the Stein kids settled on the floor.

"This is going to be easy," Barbara said. "You'll just dress up like yourselves and we'll win for sure."

Frankie said, "There are six of us in this room. Mother Scary said there can be only five winners."

"Besides," Elisa said, "is that fair?"

"Is what fair?" said Howie.

"Would it not be too easy for us to win the contest by dressing as ourselves?"

"You're right. It doesn't seem sporting," Howie said as he began to rub his chin in thought.

"Don't you guys want to win?" Barbara said.

"Think about it, Barb," Danny said. "Neither one of *us* is a monster." He was coming to realize what a drawback that could be.

"Yeah," Barbara said, suddenly looking forlorn.

"Don't worry," Danny said. "We'll think of something, and when we do, you'll be a part of it."

"Suppose I don't want to be a part of it?"

"What?" Danny was astonished.

"I've been 'Danny's little sister' for a long time. I think maybe I want to win this contest by myself. And then I'll let *you* be a part of it." She stood up and marched to the door.

"Part of what?" Danny said.

"I'll build my own monster suit and win that stupid old contest. Come on, Elisa."

"No, Barbara. If you must do this by yourself, that is the way it must be."

"Oh." A very small "oh." "Well, OK," Barbara said, and went out.

"Will she be all right?" Howie said.

"Sure," said Danny. "It's just a phase she's going through. That's what Mom and Dad always say."

"There are only five of us now," Frankie said, "but we still have no plan."

They sat for a long time thinking. It was so quiet Danny heard his mom turn the bathroom light off and walk down the hall to his parents' bedroom. He didn't know what to do. He could dress up like any monster he wanted to, but his friends had a real problem.

Then Elisa began to smile.

"What, Elisa? What?" Howie said.

"My idea is this: We will all dress up like each other."

Into the silence that followed, C.D. said, "What means this?"

"I get it!" Danny cried. "Howie can dress up like a vampire and C.D. can dress up like a werewolf. It's just like Halloween."

"This is more serious than Halloween," said Elisa.

"Capital," Howie said. He folded his arms and tried to imitate C.D. by looking serious, but when C.D. smiled in his direction, Howie collapsed into laughter.

Frankie said, "What will Elisa and I do? What will Danny do?"

Danny said, "We'll think of something, that's what we'll do."

"Very well," said Frankie. "We five will meet tomorrow at our house. I have much equipment for the making of monsters."

"I believe that," Danny said.

As he walked out of his room with his friends, Danny saw that Barbara's door was closed, and a big DO NOT DISTURB ON PAIN OF DEATH sign had been hung around the doorknob.

After Howie and C.D. and Frankie and Elisa left, Danny let Harryhausen in from the backyard. Harryhausen sniffed around as if some very interesting smells were on the floor. He followed his nose into the living room, and when he found the spot where Howie had been sitting, he whimpered and climbed onto the couch and leaned against Mr. Keegan.

"What's wrong with Harryhausen?" Mr. Keegan said.

"He probably smells that weird perfume Barbara bought at Cheapo City."

Nobody could get into Barbara's room for the rest of the day. Danny asked her how the monster costume was coming, but she would only smile. She wouldn't even let Mr. or Mrs. Keegan in for a good-night kiss. Danny asked his mom if she had any ideas how to find out what was going on.

Mrs. Keegan said, "As long as Barbara doesn't hurt

23

herself or burn down the house, I guess she has a right to her privacy.''

Danny knew his mom was right, but he couldn't help thinking that if Barbara actually won the contest then he or one of his monster friends wouldn't be able to go on Mother Scary's show.

Danny took a bus to the top of Holler Hill Drive, where the Stein mansion rambled around what looked like a grassy park. The main part of the building seemed to be made from an old windmill.

Danny used the big, heavy, monster-shaped knocker to knock on the door. Far away, in the bowels of the house, each knock echoed. A moment later there were footsteps, and the door opened with a long, dramatic creak. The creak was not quite as scary as Howie's werewolf howl, but Danny was glad it was daytime.

"Well, Danny," Mr. Stein said, and smiled. He looked a lot like Frankie, but was much taller. The knobs on his neck looked like polished brass. He was wearing a green sport shirt with a little lightning bolt sewn on the pocket and a pair of gray pants. His heavy shoes looked more like black shoe boxes.

Mr. Stein invited Danny into the bright, modern house, and put him aboard the elevator. Danny said, "Laboratory," and waved at Mr. Stein as the doors slid closed. The elevator car took him down, and a moment later Danny walked into the laboratory. It was a big room made entirely out of rocks. Strange machines, even more interesting than those in *Some Like It Scary,* lined the walls. In the ceiling over the marble slab in the center of the room was a big window. At the moment it was open to let in fresh air.

Frankie and Elisa and Howie were gathered around

the slab looking at a strange collection of stuff. There were bones and what looked like a pile of rags and a selection of bottle caps and a big white box with a red cross on it.

"Looks great," said Danny as he took his camera from a jacket pocket. "What is all this?"

"We will wait for C.D.," said Frankie.

Elisa said, "Your camera has plenty of film?"

"Twenty-four shots."

"Bully," Howie said.

A second later the elevator chimed, and C.D. entered carrying a long white box. He bowed and said, "It is a beautiful day. I would have flown, but I had this to carry." He set the box on the slab with the other stuff.

"Very well," said Elisa.

Howie said, "These are for you." He handed C.D. the pile of rags and the bones. "Put on these old, torn clothes and gnaw on these bones and you will make a first-class werewolf."

C.D. did not look happy. He clutched the clothes to his chest, but held the bones in one hand as if they were covered in slime.

"What's the matter?" Danny said.

"I did not realize being a werewolf called for such clothing and such—you will pardon me if I am frank—for such animal remains."

Howie said angrily, "The clothes have been washed and the chicken bones, are, well, just chicken bones."

"Perhaps," said Frankie, "he is used to other things."

"Yeah," said Danny, "like a tuxedo and Fluid of Life."

"Ah," said Howie, and nodded. "I see this will be a learning experience for all of us."

" 'Educational,' Ms. Cosgrove would say," said Elisa.

25

"Yes," C.D. said with some pleasure. "For instance, this, Howie, is for you."

Smiling as bravely as he could, Howie pulled the top off the white box and inside found black pants with a satin stripe down the outside of each leg, a black coat with tails and satin collar, a white shirt with fancy ruffles on the front, a wide red satin belt, and a bow tie on an elastic band.

"It is a Howie-size tuxedo," C.D. said.

"What's this?" Howie said, and held up the red satin belt.

"That is a cummerbund."

"Of course," said Howie, but he didn't look happy.

"You'll look great," Danny said.

"Indeed," C.D. said. "Keep your upper lip stiff."

"Quite," Howie said.

Danny looked at what remained on the slab and said, "Are these for me?" He picked up two of the bottle caps and held one to either side of his neck.

"Exactly," Elisa said.

Frankie pulled a cardboard box from under the slab and handed it to Danny. Inside was a simple gray jacket and a pair of enormous shoes. "This'll be great," Danny said as he pulled on the jacket. His fingertips came only to the inside of the wrists. He sat down on the stone floor and pulled on the shoes. But when he tried to walk in them, he found they were so big they slipped off.

Elisa frowned at Danny and pulled the sleeves up as if the jacket were a sweater. "And you will not have to walk in the shoes. This is good enough for a photograph."

"But the knobs won't stay on."

Elisa frowned at Danny again and rubbed her chin.

"I have some chewing gum," Howie said. He took a pack from his pocket and pulled a stick from the pack and was about to open it when Danny said, "I'd rather chew it myself, if you don't mind, Howie."

"Quite right." Howie handed the gum to Danny.

Danny chewed the gum as quickly as he could, filling his mouth with the sweet, fruity flavor. When the gum was good and soft, he pulled the gray lump from his mouth, pulled it into two pieces, and stuck one of them to the edge of one knob. He pushed the knob against his neck. The gum pulled at the tiny, invisible hairs on his neck, but it wouldn't stick.

"Hmm," they all said together.

Danny said, "My dad says that duct tape will stick to anything."

"It is well known," Frankie said, and lumbered across the laboratory to a cabinet. He pulled out electronic devices and ancient bottles covered with cobwebs. "Ah!" he said, and came back with a wide roll of gray cloth tape. Frankie tore off two narrow strips and made each strip into a small circle. Then he stuck a knob to one side of the circle and stuck the other side of the circle to Danny's neck.

"What do you think?" Danny said.

"Capital," Howie said.

"Very knoblike and convincing," C.D. said.

Frankie and Elisa just nodded.

"But what about you guys?" Danny said.

"Indeed," said C.D. "Not only must you become a different monster, you must cover up the knobs in your necks."

"It is easy," said Elisa, and opened the white box with the red cross on the side. "We have many yards of gauze," she said, and unrolled some of it. It was like thin, loosely woven white cloth—the kind of stuff that you put over your cut when you put on a Band-Aid. She reached up and began to wrap the gauze around Frankie's head.

"The Mummy!" Danny, Howie, and C.D. cried together.

"Indeed," Elisa said. "I suggest we prepare for the photograph."

They took the elevator up into the main part of the house, and each of them went into a bathroom to change into his or her monster clothes.

Danny had the easiest job. All he had to do was put on the shoes, pull up the sleeves of the coat, and attach the other knob. In the mirror, he looked pretty good. Just for good measure he combed his hair back. It stood up and made him look taller. He bared his teeth and growled like the monster in the Frankenstein movies. Not bad.

He had to shuffle back to the elevator because his feet kept lifting out of the enormous shoes if he walked the regular way.

After he got back to the laboratory he didn't have long to wait. C.D. arrived dressed in a torn shirt and short pants. He'd evidently gotten used to the bones, though he never actually got them very near his mouth. He tried to act like a dog, but he couldn't help being dignified.

Howie strode into the laboratory beaming.

"You look quite splendid," C.D. said.

Howie smiled and said, "Don't I just? Mrs. Stein helped me figure out all the strange buttons, snaps, and pins on the tuxedo. You're pretty convincing, too."

Elisa and Frankie took the longest, but waiting was worthwhile. Each of them was wrapped from head to foot in gauze, with just a slit left for eyes, nose, and

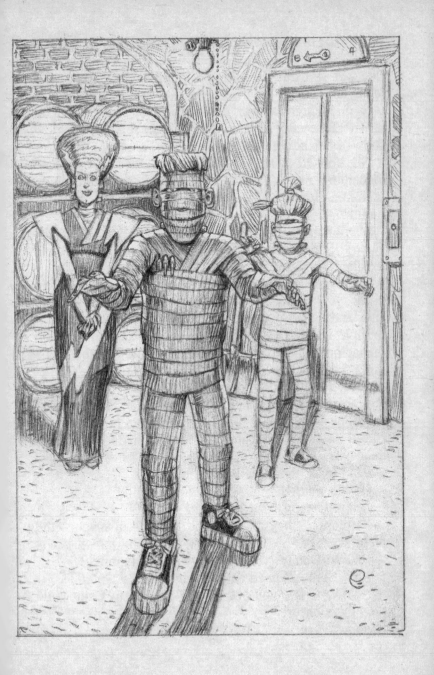

mouth. They each limped off the elevator, arms out, dragging one leg. Mrs. Stein was right behind them. She was stylishly dressed in a long red gown and had a jewel in each of the two knobs on her neck. Her hair was piled high on her head and had a lightning bolt down either side. Danny handed her his camera and showed her how to use it.

She looked at Howie critically and said, "You need something more." With a red lipstick she'd brought with her, she drew drips of blood down either side of his mouth.

"Dramatic," C.D. said, "if not entirely accurate."

Mrs. Stein nodded and said, "Are you ready for me to take the picture?"

Danny and the monster kids ran around trying different poses. At last they decided that Danny would lie on the slab and Frankie would tilt it up toward the camera. Frankie and C.D. would stand on one side of the slab menacing him. Elisa and Howie would do the same thing from the other side. They got into position.

"Ready?" Mrs. Stein said.

Frankie and Elisa raised their arms. C.D. fiddled with his bones and threw back his head to howl. Howie curled his fingers at Danny. All Danny had to do was lie there.

"Let's see those teeth, Howie."

Howie snarled.

"Say 'Creepy,' " Mrs. Stein said.

"Creepy," they all said, and Mrs. Stein snapped the picture.

"Now, Danny, you menace the two mummies."

Mrs. Stein snapped another picture.

"Now, C.D., you and Howie pretend to fight while the others cheer."

She snapped another one. Twenty-four pictures, just like that. When she was done, she handed the camera to Danny and he took out the film.

"It'll take a few days to process," Danny said.

"Nonsense," Frankie said, and took the roll of film from him. Everyone followed Frankie down into the Mad Room. It was as large as the laboratory, but very modern and brilliantly lit. Computers and video games were everywhere.

"Observe," Frankie said, and put the film into the top of a machine that looked a lot like a toaster. he closed the lid.

"The Miracle Monster Developer," Elisa said. "Frankie invented it himself."

The machine hummed for a moment, and then photographs dropped into a tray at the bottom, one by one.

"Wow," Danny said as he picked up the first one and passed it to Howie. Howie and C.D. were impressed, too. It wasn't long before they had twenty-four photos laid out on a table.

Some were disqualified right away because heads or entire bodies were chopped off by the edge of the picture. Some were too light or too dark. "Actually," said Danny, "'I like the first one the best." He tapped the one in which he was lying on the slab.

"Me, too," said Howie. And the rest of them agreed.

"We cannot lose," C.D. said.

"You have a good chance," Mrs. Stein admitted.

Danny raised the photo triumphantly and said, "I'll mail it tomorrow morning."

Chapter Four

Bats Lead to Harder Stuff

While he and Barbara were walking to school the next day, Danny dropped the Mother Scary entry into a mailbox. "What about you?" he said.

Barbara smiled a confident smile. "I have a few days yet," she said.

Before the morning bell, Danny waited for his friends under a tree in the P.S. 13 schoolyard. He saw Howie roll in at the gate on his skateboard and make a fancy racing turn as he stopped in front of Danny. Howie said, "You look normal enough again."

"I look the way I always do, anyway," Danny said.

They were soon joined by Frankie and Elisa, also dressed in their normal clothes. "It is a relief," Elisa said. "I was picking gauze from between my teeth all night."

A bat fluttered down among them, and a second later it grew into C.D. He bowed and said, "It is good to be myself again."

"That's what we were all just saying," Howie said. "But you look tired."

"This does not surprise me," he said. "Family gatherings continue till sunrise. I think I will take a bat nap before school starts." He leaped into the air and became a bat that fluttered up into the tree and hung like a tiny umbrella.

"Hey, freaks," a familiar voice called.

"Oh no," Danny said.

"It is unavoidable," Elisa said.

Stevie Brickwald approached them, followed by Jason Nickles and Angela Marconi and a few of his other friends. Jason was a terrible practical joker, and no secret was safe around Angela. Danny didn't understand how they all stood each other.

"You guys are in big trouble now," Stevie said. Suddenly a hand shot out and stuck something on Danny's shirt. Danny pulled it off and looked at it. It was a tin button that said in big red letters:

KEEP OUR HOMES SAFE.
KEEP BROOKLYN MONSTER-FREE.
MONSTER MASHERS

"What is this?" Danny said.

"This," said Stevie as if he were quoting the Pledge of Allegiance, "is the end of you graveyard googies. We're going to have all you weirdos deported."

"What does *deported* mean?"

"I know this word," Elisa said. "My parents speak of it sometimes. It means sending someone back to the country from which he came."

"Yeah," said Jason. "And you freaks are going right back to weirdo land."

Angela said, "My father says that with all the weirdos in Brooklyn, nobody's safe to walk the streets."

34

"Monster Mashers?" Danny said.

"Yeah, monster lover. Want to join?" Stevie laughed, and his friends laughed, too. When he stopped, they stopped. He spoke again. "The Monster Mashers is an organization started by that great friend of normal people everywhere, that Master Masher himself, Arthur Debarber."

From his pocket, Stevie pulled a black-and-white glossy photograph that he unfolded. Despite the cracks and seams from all the folding, it was easy for Danny to see it was a picture of a man with a wide face, a nose like a cauliflower, and thin lips that, at the moment, were shaped into a silly smirk.

The guy in the picture was wearing a uniform loaded down with yards of medals and tangles of braid. You could barely see either shoulder or his chest. On his hat was a badge that showed a witch riding a broom crash-landing into the ground.

Stevie put his hand over his heart. "What a guy that Arthur Debarber is. When I grow up, I want to be just like him."

"Me, too," said Jason.

"Me, too," said Angela.

"I'm delighted to see that all of you are thinking for yourselves," Howie said.

"You think you're pretty smart, don't you?" Stevie said, almost poking his finger into Howie's chest. Danny knew that Stevie had to be a little careful. Not only could Howie frighten Stevie with a howl, but Stevie was afraid of bats and the electricity in the Stein kids' fingers. "It just so happens," Stevie went on, "that me and the Master Masher are working on a big project right now."

Howie said, "You're crazy, Stevie. Did you know that? You and your psychotic friends are much more dangerous to Brooklyn than any real or imagined monsters.''

"Oh, yeah? If it wasn't for the Monster Mashers, monsters would murder us in our beds and suck our blood and steal our brains."

"You're safe on the brain score, anyway," Howie said.

"Huh?"

Jason got it, and he laughed. Stevie glared at Jason and went on: "It just so happens that our current crusade is to get Mother Scary off the television." He read from a sheet of paper he pulled from his pocket: " 'For being undesirable and engaging in antisocial and supernatural activities.' "

"You wouldn't deport her!" Danny cried.

Stevie just smiled.

Angela pointed up into the tree under which they were all standing. "Hey, Stevie. What's that?"

Stevie looked up and his face went slack. Then it went angry. He shook his fist at the treetop. "It's a bat." His voice got low and accusatory. "And you know what bats lead to. First you let bats hang around. The next thing you know, you got *vampires*. Something must be done." He picked up a rock. "Come on, guys, let's show 'em what we do with monsters."

Jason and Angela looked at each other. Stevie's other friends also acted uncertain. Stevie saw what was happening and said, "Or do you want monsters to bury you alive?"

Howie stepped forward and said, "You just don't like bats because you're afraid of C.D.'s pet, Spike."

"I ain't afraid of a bat or anything else," Stevie said, and cocked his arm, ready to throw.

Danny didn't like the looks of things. All the kids

36

who had arrived with Stevie were picking up rocks. He looked at Elisa and Howie, hoping one of them would have an idea, but they seemed just as shocked as he was. There had to be some way to save C.D. He was a sitting duck—er, bat. Danny took a deep breath and as loudly as he could shouted, "Pizza!"

C.D. in his bat form leaped into the air. He shrieked and flapped around the tree.

"Get 'em!" Stevie shouted, and let his rock fly. More rocks followed from his friends. But C.D. saw the rocks coming—probably with his sonar—and flew to the top of a tree at the other side of the schoolyard.

"I'm going to pulverize you," Stevie said, and came toward Danny with menace in his eyes and knuckles in his fist. Danny was too busy watching Stevie to notice if Howie was ready to howl, or if the Stein kids were ready to give Stevie an electrical zap.

"What's going on here?" Ms. Cosgrove said angrily, and hustled up between Danny and Stevie.

"I believe," Howie said, "there was a misunderstanding about the local wildlife."

Ms. Cosgrove said, "I'm glad you kids are interested in nature, but really, Stevie, you must learn to control yourself."

"Sorry, Ms. Cosgrove."

"What was the misunderstanding about, Danny?"

"Bats, I guess," Danny said miserably.

"Well," said Ms. Cosgrove brightly. "Bats are very interesting, you know. Maybe we'll see what our science book has to say about them."

The bell rang.

"All right, kids. Everybody to your classrooms, now."

Danny and his friends walked off one way. Stevie and his little gangsters walked off the other. As they walked toward the building, Howie said, "Yelling 'pizza' was a clever idea, Danny."

"No big deal. You and C.D. hate garlic so much I figured it had to work." Danny knew they didn't actually hate garlic, but it was sure to change Howie into a werewolf and C.D. into a bat. Danny shook his head and went on, "That Arthur Debarber is on the weird, freakish side himself. If he weren't so offensive, I think he would actually be interesting."

Frankie said, "It's like in the Old Country."

"Indeed," Elisa said. "In the Old Country, one angry villager could whip the rest of the villagers into a frenzy." She bit her lower lip. "I did not think this would happen in Brooklyn."

"It hasn't really happened yet," Danny said. "Stevie Brickwald has hated you guys for a long time. That's nothing new."

"'Followers are new," Frankie said.

"Besides," Danny went on, "it can't be against the law to be supernatural. A lot of people on the street are a little strange. If you started deporting all of them, Greenwich Village would be empty."

"Still," said Howie, "worse things have started with less."

Elisa nodded and said, "Howie is correct. We have learned about such things in history class. We must not wait too long to find out if Stevie and the Monster Mashers can do as they threaten. We must do something to stop them right now."

"Absolutely," Howie said. "We don't want to find out the truth the hard way."

At lunchtime, Stevie passed out bumper stickers that said, "Monster Mashers Unite!" A lot of kids took them. Even Danny took one on the theory that it was a good idea to keep track of what your enemy was doing.

Arthur Finster, a scrawny kid who'd had trouble with Stevie himself, walked over to Danny waving a bumper sticker and said, "What is this?"

"Garbage," Danny said.

"I can see that," Arthur Finster said. "What'll we do about it? I like 'Mother Scary's Matinee.' "

"Me, too. I guess all we can do is let other kids know how stupid we think Stevie is being."

"Sounds dangerous."

Danny could only agree. It looked as if, one way or another, he and his friends were going to get hurt.

When Danny got home, Barbara rushed upstairs with an armload of black cloth and some old pots from the kitchen. "What's the rush?" Danny called up the stairs after her.

"You'll see."

Danny was at the kitchen table a few minutes later when Mr. Keegan came in carrying a camera. He put it down and snagged a chocolate chip cookie from the plate in the middle of the table.

"Did you take Barbara's picture for the contest?" Danny said.

"I did." Mr. Keegan chewed for a long time.

"Well, what was she dressed as?"

Mr. Keegan swallowed what he'd been chewing and said, "I've been sworn to secrecy."

"I won't tell anybody."

"I was specifically asked to not tell you."

Danny only nodded. The way things were going, what else could he expect?

Chapter Five

Boo! From Mother Scary

The next day Barbara gave her roll of film to Elisa so that she could give it to Frankie and he could run it through his Miracle Monster Developer. The day after that, Elisa gave Barbara a small envelope. Danny knew what was in it. He offered to carry the envelope, hoping he could sneak a look at the photographs that were inside.

"No way, José," Barbara said, and walked a little faster.

She also would not let him carry the envelope that she mailed on the third day.

Furthermore, Elisa would not tell Danny or Howie or anybody else what Barbara's photographs looked like. Frankie wouldn't tell either. He said having a Miracle Monster Developer was a "sacred trust." Danny felt that he and Howie were the only two people in the world who didn't know what Barbara's big-deal costume was.

During every recess and lunch break, Stevie Brickwald

and his friends continued their antimonster campaign. They wore their buttons, and bicycles sprouted bumper stickers. Somebody even put a Monster Masher bumper sticker on Howie's skateboard, and he angrily tore it off.

It turned out that a lot of kids in Ms. Cosgrove's fifth grade class had entered the Mother Scary contest. Out on the schoolyard, Stevie called these kids disgusting, and not real kids at all, but monsters. In the classroom he said very little on the subject. And when Ms. Cosgrove said, "If any of you win the contest, I'd like you to write a report on your experience for school. For extra credit, of course," Stevie actually smiled.

"'I don't like it when he smiles," Howie said.

"Yeah," Danny said. "Anything that makes Stevie that happy has to be really awful."

"You think it has something to do with Mother Scary?"

"It wouldn't surprise me," Danny said.

It was about a week after that that Danny got his letter in the mail. The return address was "Mother Scary's Matinee," and it was written in the same spooky script that was on television. Even before he opened the envelope, he hollered "Whoopee!" and danced around so much that Harryhausen barked with excitement.

"Whoa there, cowboy," Mrs. Keegan said. "'You don't even know what the letter says."

Danny sat down at the kitchen table and carefully cut open one end of the envelope. He pulled out the letter. Instead of "Dear Danny," it said "Boo!" After that it told him he and all four of his friends had won the contest, and that they should appear at the TV station in two weeks, dressed in their monster clothes. They'd won! They'd actually won! Danny sat back in his chair, too stunned to move.

"Hadn't you better call your friends?" Mrs. Keegan said.

"Oh yeah." Danny leaped from his chair and called Howie and C.D. and the Stein kids. Even Howie was speechless.

Barbara got home a few hours later. She'd been at a Girls' Pathfinders meeting and had hand-sewn together a leather pen-and-pencil holder that she was very proud of. But she forgot all about it when Mrs. Keegan handed her a letter.

"What is it?" Danny said.

"It's from 'Mother Scary's Matinee,' " cried Barbara, delighted.

"It might not be what you think it is," Danny said, trying to soften the blow that was sure to come. Mother Scary had said there would be five winners, and he and his friends were already them.

With much less care than Danny had used, Barbara tore her envelope open and read the letter inside.

She looked at her mother and said, "It says that I won a special prize for ingenuity. What's ingenuity?"

"Creative thinking," Mrs. Keegan said.

Barbara read on. "It says here that I can come down to the Mother Scary show along with the first-prize winners."

Barbara hopped around with the letter, singing a camp song she'd learned in the Girls' Pathfinders. It was about wishing she were in Dixie, but it seemed to fit her mood.

When Barbara had calmed down a little, Danny said, "That must have been one terrific costume."

"It had ingenuity," Barbara said proudly.

"What exactly was it?"

Barbara looked away with her nose in the air.

"Go ahead and show it to us," Mrs. Keegan said. "There's no reason to keep it a secret. You can't do better than win."

"OK," said Barbara. "I'll show you one of the reject pictures." And she ran out of the kitchen, leaving Danny and his mother to wonder what the costume was.

"Here," said Barbara, and thrust a snapshot into Danny's hand. There was Barbara, dressed in a long black dress and a pointed hat. A soup pot was on her bed, and she was stirring whatever was in it with the handle of a broom.

Danny said, "You dressed like Mother Scary."

"Ingenuity," Barbara said, and tapped her forehead.

Danny had to admit that was pretty good, though sharing the spotlight with his sister had not been what he'd had in mind when all this began.

Howie made the announcement the next day during Show-and-Tell. The class went wild, and Ms. Cosgrove had trouble restoring order. Some members of the class cheered and seemed as genuinely delighted as the winners themselves. Others, obviously poor losers, grumbled that it was unfair, because Danny's friends were monsters to begin with and had a head start. Stevie and his friends seemed unaccountably delighted. At recess, Stevie swaggered over to the monster kids where they were standing under their usual tree, and he said, "You dorks have a real surprise coming."

"Your family is perhaps moving to another state?" C.D. said.

"Somebody'll be moving. That's for sure." Stevie laughed and stuck a bumper sticker onto Frankie's shirt. He ran off, still laughing.

"I wish he would spring his trap," Howie said. "He's making me nervous."

"I have a feeling," Frankie said, "we will find out soon enough." He tore the bumper sticker off his shirt, wadded it up, and threw it into a trash can.

"The night we're on 'Mother Scary's Matinee'?" Danny said.

Elisa said, "It would be like Stevie to attempt to ruin something for everybody all at once."

Chapter Six

A Surprise Guest

Mrs. Keegan made spaghetti the afternoon Danny and Barbara and the others were to be on "Mother Scary's Matinee." At Danny's special request, she left out the garlic she normally put in. She said, "Can't have Howie and C.D. having allergy attacks on a big day like this."

When Danny locked him outside, Harryhausen scratched at the kitchen door and cried. But when Howie and C.D. showed up, he stopped immediately and settled down in front of his doghouse.

After lunch, Frankie and Elisa wrapped each other in gauze. C.D. went up to Danny's room, where the two of them put on their costumes. C.D. looked a lot more comfortable as a werewolf than he had before. He even twirled the chicken bones in the air like drumsticks. Danny had to stuff newspaper into the enormous shoes so that he could walk in them without shuffling. Mr. and Mrs. Keegan both helped Howie recall the mysteries of his tuxedo.

When everyone was gathered in front of the front

door, Frankie said, "Barbara, are you wearing your perfume again?"

"Of course. This is a special occasion." Barbara smoothed her black dress and adjusted her pointy hat to be a little more crooked. "I didn't spend an entire dollar at Cheapo City for nothing."

They piled into the Keegan's station wagon, and while Mr. Keegan drove to the television station, Barbara tried to teach everybody the song about wanting to be in Dixie. Danny was in such a good mood he didn't even mind, and sang along with everybody else as they rolled along.

Mr. Keegan pulled into the driveway at the television station and told the guard who they were. The guard looked in at them, grinning, and told Mr. Keegan where to park. They were all quiet as Mr. Keegan drove among enormous buildings, each one much larger than the P.S. 13 auditorium.

"Here we are," said Mrs. Keegan as Mr. Keegan pulled into his spot and turned off the engine. Immediately Danny and the others piled out of the car. "Hurry, hurry," said Barbara.

"There's plenty of time," Mrs. Keegan said, looking at the letters she carried. "Stage Five, it says."

"This is Stage Seven," Elisa said, and pointed at the big brown sign painted on the wall.

"And there is Stage Six," said C.D., as he pointed at the next building down.

Danny found that he couldn't run very well in his big shoes, even with the newspaper stuffed into them, so he walked with his parents while Barbara and his friends ran ahead to Stage 5.

A door that took up most of one enormous wall was open, and the group stood outside it looking in. Most of

Stage 5 was empty space. There were chalk marks on the floor, and flat wall things—as if somebody had collapsed a regular house like an accordion—leaning in a rack. Nobody seemed to be around, but Danny heard voices coming from somewhere.

"We can't stand out here all day," Howie said, and strode into the stage, looking magnificent in his tuxedo. The rest of them followed him to where the voices came from.

It was a corner of the studio made up to look like Mother Scary's forest. In front of a black backdrop with stars pasted on it were some scraggly trees—almost branches, really—held upright on wooden stands. In front of that was Mother Scary's cauldron, which at the moment had a plastic foam cup floating in it. The whole Mother Scary area wasn't much bigger than the bathroom Danny shared with Barbara at home.

Facing this set were two big cameras, some folding chairs, and a big square television. Cables as big around as fire hoses came from the cameras and went into a big box full of wires. Elisa had a difficult time keeping Frankie's hands off it. Although the television was plugged into the same box, nothing was on it at the moment except a test pattern with a profile of an Indian in the middle.

A woman in a Mother Scary costume was talking to a couple of guys dressed in blue jeans and work shirts. One of them wore a headset with earphones and a little microphone hanging off it. Danny studied the woman closely. She didn't look scary. She just looked like an old Gypsy woman wearing too much makeup.

"Zelda Bella?" Howie said. He almost whispered, but the sound carried in that big, empty room.

The woman in the Mother Scary costume turned to

look at Howie. She looked at all of them, and grinned. "Say," she said, "aren't you the kid who wanted to be a real boy?"

Howie acted as if he'd been caught at something he shouldn't be doing. He said, "As a matter of fact, I am."

"How'd that turn out?"

"Just fine, actually."

Zelda Bella's eyes widened in surprise. She scratched the back of her neck and shrugged as she said, "I knew it would. Fruit is good for you. It always works."

"We have won your contest," C.D. said, and bowed.

Zelda Bella gave an awkward bow back and said, "I bet you did. And no wonder in those getups."

"And I won the special prize for ingenuity," Barbara said.

"Oh yeah. I heard about you," Zelda Bella said, and laughed so loud the sound seemed to fill the stage. "What's that smell?"

"Eau de Springtime," Howie said.

"Strong stuff. It must have cost plenty," Zelda Bella said. "Tom, come on over here. I want you to meet a few friends of mine."

Tom was the man without the headset. He was the director of "Mother Scary's Matinee." "One of the names at the end of the show that nobody reads," he said, laughing good-naturedly.

Tom got them to wait just outside the Mother Scary area. Each of them got to sit in a folding chair that had the word *guest* stenciled on the back. A woman came by and extracted the cup from the cauldron. She came back a few minutes later and threw chunks of ice into the cauldron. The ice made the water bubble and give off smoke.

"Neat," Barbara said.

"Dry ice," Frankie said. "Very cold. Colder than regular ice. Made from compressed carbon dioxide."

Pretty soon another guy wearing jeans, this one with a beard, arrived. He was the second cameraman. He put on a headset, too. Hot, bright lights came on, illuminating the Mother Scary set, and somebody pushed the big door closed with a *whumph*. They were in a little island of light in the big, dark room.

It wasn't long before Tom called out "Quiet on the set," and began counting down: "Five . . . four . . . three . . . two . . . one." He pointed at a guy sitting in front of a machine. The guy pushed a slider and the Mother Scary theme music came through speakers in the ceiling high above them.

Danny had trouble deciding whether he should watch Mother Scary live, right there in front of him, or on the television. It was interesting looking first one place and then the other, to see the differences in how Mother Scary and her set looked.

Mother Scary made some jokes about a rubber mouse, and talked a little about the winners of the contest— "Who will be with us later," she said. Everybody in the guest chairs squirmed with happiness. Then she made some magic dirt—"Iron filings," Frankie said—spell out the name of the movie. It was *Arm-wrestling Women from the Moon*.

A commercial for Wonky Wheats came on the television.

"OK," said Tom. "You can talk now if you want to."

"*Arm-wrestling Women from the Moon* is a classic," Mr. Keegan said.

Mrs. Keegan looked at him, astonished, and said, "You can't be serious."

"Hey, guys," Danny said "let's do the old Mother Scary Salute."

"Great idea," Mr. Keegan said.

"You're as bad as the children," Mrs. Keegan said, and chuckled.

"Watch this. OK, kids, on my count of three." Mr. Keegan counted to three and then raised both hands. He shook them in the air while he cried "Boo!" and then cackled like a witch.

Zelda Bella only glanced at them and waved, but the cameraman with the beard made the salute back at them.

"Aaiiee!" somebody back in the darkness cried. A moment later a man in a uniform dripping with braid and medals marched into the light. He was carrying something that looked like a flashlight with a pie plate taped to the front and wire wrapped around the body. Danny recognized him immediately. The man shook a finger under Zelda Bella's nose and said, "I am Arthur Debarber, the Master Masher of the Monster Mashers. Look how you are corrupting the youth of Brooklyn with your monster motions." He pointed to Danny and the others in the guest chairs.

Zelda Bella seemed so astonished she could not say anything. It wouldn't have done her any good to try, because Arthur Debarber went on. "With my magic sensor," he said as he shook his flashlight dingus, "I will sense any magic you use, and prove beyond a particle of a doubt that you, Mother Scary, are really a witch and should be deported back to whatever vile hole you come from."

"Rumania is not a vile hole," Zelda Bella said, pretty calmly under the circumstances.

Frankie whispered, "That is no sensor of magic. It is junk."

52

Arthur Debarber went on. "I am only awaiting certain evidence before I make my case to the public and see that you and all monsters like you are banished from Brooklyn forever!"

Tom said, "Who is this nut? Has anyone called studio security?"

"No need," Arthur Debarber said. He stomped across the dark stage. There was a crash as he ran into the rack of wall things, and then a small, regular-size door opened. He cast a long shadow back at them as he went out. The shadow looked to Danny like a dagger.

"My goodness," Mrs. Keegan said. "The last time I saw a guy like him it was in a World War Two newsreel."

Zelda Bella said, "What set that guy off?"

"We were doing the old Mother Scary Salute," Danny said.

"Is that what that was?" she said.

"It's from the old Mother Scary show when my dad was a kid."

"Didn't you watch Mother Scary when you were young?" Mr. Keegan said.

"They didn't carry the show in Rumania, I guess. That nut seemed to know what it was, though. It made him angry enough."

"Yes," said Howie. "It's interesting, isn't it?"

"You have a plan?" Frankie said.

Howie looked uncertain. "Perhaps a plan for a plan."

"He might be getting his certain evidence pretty soon," Danny said.

Mr. Keegan said, "You kids stay away from that guy. He's crazy. Look, the movie's starting."

Everybody watched the movie on the television, but Danny wasn't thinking about it. He suspected that none of his friends was either.

*   *   *

Arthur Debarber had not succeeded in putting a damper on the day. *Arm-wrestling Women from the Moon* was such an ostentatiously terrible movie it couldn't help putting you in a good mood. Mother Scary pretended she was frightened as she introduced each of the contest winners. She let Barbara stir her cauldron.

When the show was over, somebody rolled back the enormous door, letting in the late afternoon sunshine. Mr. and Mrs. Keegan strolled slowly back to the car while the kids talked to Zelda Bella and got autographs.

"What do you think of Arthur Debarber?" Elisa said.

Zelda Bella looked as if she felt something awful creeping up her back when she said, "I don't want to go back to Rumania. I haven't been there since I was a kid."

C.D. said, "We must do something. He collects more followers all the time. His certain evidence will come soon."

Zelda Bella glanced around and lowered her voice. "Look, kids; you take my home address and phone number. Let's stay in touch, huh?"

Using one finger, Frankie typed Zelda Bella's address and phone number into his homemade portable electronic calculator/dictionary/address book.

"Come on, kids," Mrs. Keegan called.

And they all ran for the car.

Chapter Seven

Certain Evidence

Most of Sunday, Danny worked on his report about "Mother Scary's Matinee." He left out all the parts about Arthur Debarber. There was no point giving the guy free publicity.

On Monday, he and the other monster kids turned in their reports. At recess, Stevie seemed to have more kids following him around than ever. Some of them weren't even in Ms. Cosgrove's class. He sneered at Danny and said, "That witch and your goofball friends aren't long for this borough, boy."

"Yeah," his friends called out in support.

"You just wait," Danny said, and wished he knew what they should wait for. Stevie enjoyed that for a moment, then strutted off, his mob in train. "Hey, wait," Danny said.

Stevie turned slowly and said, "What?"

"Got one of those Monster Masher bumper stickers?"

"What's it to you?"

Carefully Danny said, "Oh. It'll just give me something to think about."

Stevie chuckled evilly and handed him a sticker before he walked away.

Danny ran to where his friends were waiting under their tree. "Look what I have," Danny said.

"Trash," C.D. said.

"No. Look." Danny pointed to tiny type at the bottom of the bumper sticker. It gave the address of the Monster Masher offices.

"So what?" said Howie.

"I see what Danny is thinking," Elisa said. "We will go there and study the enemy."

"Exactly," Danny said. "I'll call my mom and ask her to call all of yours. We'll be a little late getting home from school."

"Excellent," Howie said. C.D., Elisa, and Frankie nodded.

The Monster Mashers office was in a building across town. It took most of an hour to get there by bus. As they rode, the streets changed. They were not dangerous, exactly, but certainly less neat than the streets Danny and his friends were used to.

They got off the bus, and Danny saw a newspaper blowing down the street like some alien animal on the prowl. The buildings around them were too new to be as charming as the ones in C.D.'s neighborhood, but old enough to look broken-in. Very broken-in, perhaps. A lot of people were on the streets. And while some of them looked a bit threadbare, they hustled along as if they had somewhere to go.

"Here we are," Frankie said.

They looked up at a white stone pile that rose many floors to a spire. "No wonder they call it 'the Pointy Building,'" said Howie. And, indeed, that was the name carved in stone over the door.

The lobby of the Pointy Building was large and cold and covered in butterscotch-colored marble. Stone angels looked down at them from ceiling corners. They found the directory and looked for Monster Mashers among the private eyes, souvenir supply companies, artists, music teachers, and coin-collecting shops that inhabited the building. Monster Mashers was on the fourth floor.

"What if he is not here?" C.D. said.

"I'd rather he weren't, actually," Howie said.

"What if he recognizes us from the Mother Scary show?" Danny said.

In a hopeful voice, Frankie said, "We were in costume."

Elisa said, "In any case, we have not come this far just to go back."

They rode in an elevator that clanked and wheezed as it rose slowly in the shaft. At the fourth floor the door cranked itself open and they stepped into a long brown hallway with shadows at each end. A radio in one of the offices was whispering rock and roll.

Each of the doors had a yellow glass window that you couldn't see through because it was pebbled, like the glass in a bathroom window. Some of the doors had no names on them, and even some of the ones that did seemed to have nothing behind them but silence and time and dust.

"Here it is," Elisa said. "Do we knock?"

Danny looked back along the hall and said, "It doesn't say to knock. Some of the other doors did."

"You go in first," C.D. said.

Danny looked at Howie. Howie nodded, so Danny opened the door and went in. The room was empty except for a beat-up coffee table with ancient magazines on it. Nobody was at the desk. A Monster Mashers bumper sticker was thumbtacked to the wall behind it. "Hello?" Howie called.

"Hello?" somebody called back from down a short hall. They heard the squeak of somebody pushing back a chair and standing up. "Hello," said the man who walked along the hall to the front office. It was Arthur Debarber, still in his uniform. He smiled pleasantly and said, "What can I do for you kids?"

"Uh," said Danny, thinking fast, "we want to hear all about the Monster Mashers."

"You couldn't find a better cause. Come on." He walked back the way he'd come and motioned them to follow. He turned once and said, "Don't I know you?" and peered at them.

"We have not had the pleasure," Elisa said.

That seemed to satisfy him because he ushered them into a big square room with tall windows that let in sunlight. Against one wall was a desk covered with newspapers and magazines. A long table ran down the center of the room. On it was a curious collection of things.

"I suppose you don't believe in witches and monsters," Arthur Debarber said as he sat down behind his desk and folded his hands.

"We could not say," C.D. said, not quite injuring the truth.

Arthur Debarber sprang to his feet and said, "I have proof. Proof!" He walked to the long table and stood by the first thing. It was a small cardboard box with a couple of teeth in it. They looked like bait for the Tooth Fairy, just normal teeth, and not very monstrous. "This," Arthur Debarber said, "is a collection of werewolf teeth."

Howie studied the teeth closely, politely said "I see," and put them down.

The next item Arthur Debarber showed them was a bottle of pink water labeled WITCH'S BREW. It looked a lot like pale pink water. He had a rock from Bald Mountain, said to be the site of witch conventions. Danny hefted it in one hand. It was just a rock. He'd seen more interesting ones at the Bronx Botanical Garden.

"What's this?" Elisa said, and held up a photograph of a calico kitten. The kitten was cute and fuzzy and looked entirely harmless.

"This," said Arthur Debarber, "is perhaps the most diabolical exhibit of them all. This is a witch's helper, her familiar."

"How can you tell?"

"All cats are familiars. I hate cats."

"Can't argue with that," Howie said.

"What's a 'Witch-o-matic'?" Frankie said, and pointed to a microwave oven on a table under the windows.

Arthur Debarber laughed and said, "Microwaving is so much more practical than burning at the stake."

Danny was horrified, and he could see by the way they drew back that the others were, too.

"Oh, it's just a joke," Arthur Debarber said, waving the horror away with one hand. "It's just the office microwave. I warm my lunch with it."

"Heh heh," said C.D weakly. "Very good." He made sucking motions with his mouth, but he did not pull his Fluid of Life from his cape. Just as well, Danny thought.

The office door opened and slammed. Somebody ran along the hallway. A breathless voice cried, "I have it, sir," and a second later Stevie Brickwald was standing in the doorway holding a manila envelope. He said, "What are you creeps doing here?"

"You know these children?" Arthur Debarber said.

61

"Yeah," said Stevie as if he were revealing a fact previously unknown to science. "They're in my class at school. And they're monsters."

"How can you tell?" said Arthur Debarber.

"Well, just look at them," Stevie said.

Danny and his friends shuffled their feet as Arthur Debarber studied them from where he stood. He said, "I'm sure you're mistaken, Stevie. Monsters are big and hairy and they have terrible teeth and bad breath. What do you have for me there?"

Stevie sputtered hopelessly for a moment, then his face broke out—that was the phrase—into a smile as he handed the envelope to Arthur Debarber, who opened it eagerly. He skimmed the top sheet of the short stack inside and said, "This is it."

"Is what?" said Danny.

"It is the certain evidence I've been waiting for. One of the technicians at the TV station snuck it out to me. It is Mother Scary's special effects budget. All she's ever spent is thirty-five cents a week on dry ice." He spoke triumphantly.

"Meaning what?" Elisa said.

Stevie said, "Meaning, you bucket of bolts, that all the magic Mother Scary does must be real. She's a real witch. She's just earned a one-way ticket to Rumania." Stevie was so happy he couldn't stand still.

"Stevie's right," Arthur Debarber said. He put the envelope down and rubbed his hands together. "With these documents in my possession, Mother Scary is doomed. Next week will be her final performance!"

"Great," said Danny. The smile on his face had no more life than a brown autumn leaf.

Chapter Eight

Thirteen Wimp Witches

The sun was touching the horizon when they morosely walked out of the Pointy Building. Each of them had dark thoughts. They did not look at each other. They somehow made it to the bus and waited for it and got on when it came. They found seats in the back.

"Can he do it?" C.D. said as the bus bounced along.

"There are many stupid people in the world," Elisa said.

Danny said, "Suppose she really is a witch?"

"Suppose she is. She has rights like anybody else. It's one of the traditions your country got from England," Howie said proudly.

"He can cause trouble anyway. I've seen it happen."

"Banned books," Frankie said. "Outlawed popular music."

"We must call Zelda Bella," Elisa said.

They rode in silence to Howie's apartment building, the Talbot Arms. It rose like a white stone ghost in the thickening gloom of twilight. Howie nodded to the doorman, and led his friends through the lobby. They rode the elevator to the top floor and got off.

Danny liked the Wolfner apartment. It was paneled in wood and had brass lamps that lit rooms with a warm glow. On the walls were big paintings of hunting scenes.

They found Mr. Wolfner in the kitchen pounding meat with a square mallet. "Just doing a little tenderizing," he said, and smacked the meat another good one as if he were swatting a fly. He glared at it as if he thought it might try to get away. Mr. Wolfner was a short, square man with a wide face. His red hair was thinning a little at the top. At the moment he was wearing an apron that said "It's a dog-eat-dog world" and showed a drawing of a happy dog eating a hot dog.

"Where's Mum?" Howie said.

"In her office doing calculations. She's asked not to be disturbed."

"Right. We're just going to use the phone."

"You know where we keep it," Mr. Wolfner said, and smacked the meat again.

Howie used the phone in the living room. He sat down on a padded bench and called the number Frankie brought up on his pocket directory. Though the conversation Howie had with Zelda Bella was short, Danny and the others waited impatiently, scratching themselves and shuffling their feet and looking at the pictures on the walls.

"That's it," Howie said as he hung up the phone. "She wants us to visit as soon as possible. There are some people she wants us to meet."

C.D. stopped sucking on his Fluid of Life long enough to say, "She told us she now lives at a place called Halloween Acres. I am most curious."

"You'll have your chance to see it tomorrow after school."

*   *   *

As Mr. Keegan drove him home from the Wolfners', Danny wondered if they weren't worried about nothing. He said, "Dad, you remember that guy at the Mother Scary show?"

"The nut?"

"Yeah. You think he's really dangerous?"

"He could be if enough people believe he's doing the right thing."

"How many is enough?"

"Hard to say. Depends on how much noise each of them makes. I guess he has the same chances as anybody else."

Not if Danny and his friends had anything to say about it.

Halloween Acres was at the end of the bus line, out where Long Island began to get wild. It was a co-op for retired people. But instead of everybody living in one building, Halloween Acres sprawled in a number of small buildings dotted around a parkland as if each one had been dropped at random by a giant child. Cats of all colors and sizes wandered the winding cement paths between the buildings. A cauldron hung over a barbecue pit surrounded by trees and picnic benches.

When Howie knocked on Zelda Bella's door, she opened it only as far as the chain would let her and looked out. Quickly she closed the door and then opened it wide. "Come in. Come in," she said, looking furtively from side to side before she closed the door behind them.

Once inside the apartment, Danny could almost believe he was back in Zelda Bella's old home behind the fruit store. This new place was bigger and seemed to have

65

more air in it, mostly because of the sliding glass door at one end of the room. Through it Danny could see a putting green where, at the moment, two thin old men in colorful clothes were tapping golf balls with clubs.

Still, the furniture was the same—old and clunky. Strange objects of bone, glass, and clay stood on tables that had the feet of animals. A loud old clock in the corner made the sound of infinity itself as it slowly ticked.

Zelda Bella said, "I want you kids to meet everybody." She introduced them to twelve women, each of whom was old enough to be Danny's grandmother. Some of them wore running suits, and others had on dresses, but they were all perky old ladies, alert as birds. Even C.D was overwhelmed by the number of strangers; he bowed, but he didn't attempt to kiss everybody's hand. "These are the kids I was telling you about," Zelda Bella said.

A large woman with a cloud of red hair so pale it was almost pink smiled politely and said, "I'm sure they're wonderful children, Zelda, but how do you know they're not, you know—"

"Ida means they might be spies for the Monster Mashers," broke in a thin woman who seemed to be conversing with a corner of the ceiling.

"They're not spies," Zelda Bella said. "These kids and I go way back. Besides, this one's a werewolf." She put a hand on Howie's shoulder. "Or he was, anyway."

"It is a private matter," Howie said.

"That's all right, honey," another woman said as she wrung her hands. She was tall and bony and had skin dark and smooth as old leather. "We're all witches."

In his mind, Danny saw flashes of Hansel and Gretel being fattened up for the oven in the witch's gingerbread house, of the Wicked Witch of the West chasing Dorothy across Oz, of all the nasty old women who'd ever troubled a fairy tale. He'd gotten used to werewolves and vampires and people bolted together from bits. They almost seemed normal. But witches were something else again. He hoped none of them offered him gingerbread.

"We will not get anywhere without trust," Frankie said.

"He speaks the truth," C.D. said. "Perhaps Howie and I can demonstrate our good faith. Have you any garlic?"

"What do you think, Howie?" Danny said.

"I suppose it is for a good cause."

Danny shrugged and said, "'Bring on the garlic."

The thin woman stood up, but Zelda Bella pushed her back onto the couch. "I'll get it, Ruth. You might come back with tulip bulbs." The women laughed understandingly and Ruth's face reddened.

There was a lot of crashing and banging in the kitchen. When it got quiet, Howie began scratching himself as if crawling with ants, and he grumbled, "This is stupid stuff. We can't deal with Arthur Debarber by committee." C.D. said nothing, but he looked around nervously.

Seconds later, Zelda Bella returned with cloves of garlic in her hand. Howie cried, "I don't know why we bother!" as he hunkered down on all fours, and hair grew down to his eyebrows. His nose lengthened and the tip darkened. He howled, and all the cats in the complex began to sing like hundreds of out-of-tune violins.

At that same moment C.D. drew his cape around him and shouted, "The vampire's main strength is that no one believes in him!" He snapped open his cape, leaped into the air, and shut up like a telescope. Where he had been was a bat flapping in circles.

The women shrieked and climbed up on the furniture and buried their heads in pillows. Howie ran around the room, howling and leaping over things, while C.D. flapped against the walls like a moth trying to escape through a windowpane.

Danny took the garlic from Zelda Bella's open hand and threw it out the sliding door. Instantly Howie and C.D. became less frantic. C.D. alighted on one end of the couch and became himself sitting there with his legs crossed. He shook his head violently, as if to clear it, and began sucking hungrily on his Fluid of Life. Howie slunk off behind a chair, curled up, and went to sleep.

Trying to catch her breath, Zelda Bella said, "Pretty convincing, don't you think, girls?"

"What about the other three?" Ida said as she settled back into her chair.

"I will vouch for them," C.D. said.

Elisa explained that Howie would sleep for a few minutes. Rather than decide anything without him, Zelda Bella proposed they have refreshments. She went into the kitchen and returned with a plate of cookies.

"Gingerbread?" Danny asked warily.

"Chocolate chip oatmeal," Zelda Bella said. "Martha made them."

A short, round woman with red cheeks waved shyly.

When Howie awoke and had a cookie, he obviously felt better. "We need a plan," he said.

Ida said, "Come on, girls. We're witches. This should be easy."

Ruth said, "A curse is always nice."

"Oh, yes," said the dark, bony woman eagerly. "We could make Arthur Debarber break out into a terrible rash. It could say"— she blocked out the words in the air with one hand—" 'Take a Monster to Lunch.' "

68

"I like that," Ida said. "Or we could change him into a cockroach." She laughed, thinking about it. It was a real laugh, not a cackle.

"Or we could turn the gasoline in his automobile into apple cider," another witch said, causing everyone to laugh even harder.

Zelda Bella said, "I don't know about you girls, but I haven't flung a curse in . . ." She thought for a moment. "I do believe I've never flung a curse. Love potions are more my line."

It seemed that none of them had ever flung a curse or changed anybody into a bug.

"We don't even fly on our broomsticks much," the bony lady said. "A lot of us are afraid of heights."

Danny nodded. This was great. He had worried before that these witches would hurt him. *Now* he worried that they couldn't even defend themselves. This was all getting to be pretty confusing.

"Well," said a lady who looked like George Washington, "I think we should write a strong letter to the local paper."

"Oh no, Norma." Ruth smiled impishly. "Let's festoon his trees with toilet paper." That got a laugh, but nobody agreed to actually do it. "Or soap the windows of his car," she said, and waited for another laugh, this time in vain.

"I think," the bony woman said, "we should follow him around till he does something really terrible, and then report him to the police."

After that it got so quiet Danny could hear the sound of one of the men outside tapping his golf ball.

"Is that all?" Howie said.

The old ladies looked at each other and then at their feet. Zelda Bella said, "I'm glad those Horrorifics you told me about aren't here to see what wimp witches we are.''

"You are not wimps," Elisa said. "You are merely sweet ladies with no experience fighting evil. I like you the way you are.''

"Here here!" cried Howie.

"Thank you," said Zelda Bella. "But that doesn't solve our problem.''

Frankie said, "Who are these Horrorifics?"

"Why," said Ida with surprise "they are Mother Scary's oldest fans. Some of them are old enough to remember when the original Mother Scary just told ghost stories on the radio.''

"Do they still meet?" Frankie said.

"Every Wednesday night since 1934," Ida said.

"We must have their address.''

"An idea?" C.D. said.

"A notion," Frankie said. "It will be an idea when it grows up.''

Chapter Nine

The Horrorifics

On the bus home from Halloween Acres, Howie said, "I don't know what we want with those old Horrorifics geezers."

"Old geezers know many things," C.D. said, and winked.

Frankie said, "Arthur Debarber got upset by the old Mother Scary Salute. Perhaps someone at the Horrorifics knew Arthur Debarber long ago."

"My dad was a member of the Mother Scary Fan Club, and he didn't know him," Danny said.

"No," said Elisa, "but your father is only one man. And Ida said that the Horrorifics did not mix with the younger fans in the Mother Scary Fan Club. The Horrorifics may have known Arthur Debarber while the fan club did not."

"And," said C.D., "if the Horrorifics are still meeting even now, after all this time, they are probably fanatics who know many things about Mother Scary, her life and times, that other people would consider trivial."

"You are hoping," Elisa said to her brother, "that they can perhaps explain the origin of Arthur Debarber's dislike of monsters?"

"I hope," Frankie said.

"Personally," Howie said, "I think we'd have more luck festooning his trees with toilet paper."

"Perhaps." Frankie smiled, which for him was like anybody else rolling on the floor with laughter. He went on: "Perhaps. But we have a larger problem. Ida said the meeting always starts at eight P.M. This is too late for me to be out alone."

"I'll talk to my dad," Danny said. "When he finds out about the Horrorifics, he'll take us to the meeting just to have an excuse to take himself."

Dinner was already in progress when Danny got home. He hurriedly washed his hands and returned to the dinner table, where he lit into his pot roast with a will. Before his mother could remind him that she worried about him when he was late, Danny said, "Me and the guys were visiting Mother Scary, you know?"

"You must have had a lot to talk about," Mrs. Keegan said, raising an eyebrow in his direction.

"I'm sorry. It just sorta got late."

"You'll have to be more responsible if you want to go visiting after school."

"You're right, Mom. But you know the interesting thing we found out? We found out about an old Mother Scary fan club called the Horrorifics."

"Oh?" Mr. Keegan said. He had a ragged chunk of pot roast on his fork, but he had evidently forgotten about it.

"Yeah. Some of them remember when Mother Scary was on the radio."

"I didn't know she was ever on the radio," Mr. Keegan said.

"Yeah. And they have meetings every Wednesday night at eight P.M. Me and the guys were thinking about going."

"Me, too," Barbara said.

Mrs. Keegan said, "Me-too had better finish her peas or she won't be going anywhere."

"You can't be out that late without a grown-up," Mr. Keegan said, and put the chunk of pot roast into his mouth.

"Oh yeah," said Danny, and waited.

"All right," said Mr. Keegan. "Call your friends and see if they want to come with us."

"That's great, Dad."

"Me, too," Barbara said.

"I thought you wanted to see the 'Snuggly Mutt' special on TV tomorrow night," Mrs. Keegan said. "You've been waiting for it for weeks."

"We could tape it," Barbara said.

Mrs. Keegan said, "We're not taping another thing till you watch some of the tapes you've already made. You must have hundreds."

"Thousands," Danny said, and Barbara poked at him with her glance.

Barbara struggled with her dilemma, and at last the Snuggly Mutts won. Danny knew it would. Barbara loved cartoons about those cute wrinkled plush animals.

School was mostly a matter of staying out of the way of Stevie Brickwald and his followers. Danny and his friends succeeded, though Stevie would never know how many times he was almost zapped with electricity by one of the Steins.

At dinner, Barbara talked of nothing but the relative merits of various Snuggly Mutt TV episodes, and Danny let her talk. Anything to keep her from asking again to go to the Horrorifics meeting.

Mr. Keegan and Danny collected the monster kids, and the car got rowdier with every stop. If Mr. Keegan hadn't been driving the car, anyone watching might have thought he was just a big kid.

The Horrorifics meeting was in the public meeting room of a local park. It was not quite eight o'clock, but there were a lot of old guys sitting around outside the room, talking and arguing. Some of them wore ties and conservative suits. Others looked as if they'd just walked off the street in the neighborhood of the Pointy Building. Everybody mixed pretty well. A dress code didn't seem to be important to this group.

Rows of folding chairs were set up inside the room, and about half of them were filled. Mr. Keegan looked around, taking it all in. Just inside the door was a guy who hadn't shaved much lately. Sparse white hair was pushed back from his forehead and fell around his ears.

"First time?" he said.

"For all of us, yes," Mr. Keegan said.

"Sign here," the man said. "You get three free meetings. Then death does not release you." He didn't even smile.

C.D. said, "You are a vampire?"

The man looked confused for a moment, then said, "Absolutely." He folded his arms, and in a thick Transylvanian accent said, "Children of the night. What music *they* make."

C.D. was going to comment on that, but Mr. Keegan dragged him to where Danny and the others were already seated.

Soon after eight, an enormous guy dressed in jeans and a T-shirt that said I GLOW IN THE DARK waddled to the front of the room and started the meeting with the old Mother Scary Salute. Then there was a lot of spirited discussion about dues and where the next Horrorifics convention would be held.

When it came time for new business, Howie raised his hand, attracting a lot of interest from the other members. The chairman called on him, and Howie said, "My friends and I are delighted to be at your meeting. We have come seeking information."

"What's going on?" Mr. Keegan whispered to Danny.

Danny whispered back, "We're doing a favor for Mother Scary."

Mr. Keegan nodded. Danny was certain there would be more questions when they got home.

"What kind of information?" the chairman said.

"Do any of you know a person named Arthur Debarber?"

There was a lot of grumbling, and Danny heard more than one of the men say that it was a shame poor old Arthur had gone bad. A very thin man, hunched like a vulture, stood up and said, "Last I saw Arthur, he was nutso-cuckoo. He'd lost all interest in old horror movies except to attack them."

"We were more interested in what Arthur was like before . . . er, his conversion."

The very thin man shrugged, hunching his shoulders even higher. He said, "He used to be one of the few kids who appreciated the classic horror stories and the traditional approaches to moviemaking. Not like these kids today, with their spatter and their gore and their special effects." He looked as if he were searching for a place to spit. Around him, men loudly agreed with him.

75

While the man had been talking, Howie made his way to the front of the room, and now he strolled up and back like a lawyer addressing the jury. Danny had seen this kind of thing lots of times on TV.

"That's very interesting," Howie said. "Do you know what changed him?"

Grumbling began again. Now a tall man wearing a suit stood up. He adjusted his glasses and said, "Well, ya know, I think it was *The Hand of Irving*—which as we know is the English-language version of the French classic *Forty-seven Blank Faces*. It was *The Hand of Irving* that pushed old Arthur over the edge."

C.D. stood up, but still could not see over the heads of those around him, so Mr. Keegan helped him up onto a chair. C.D. bowed and said, "You mean he saw this production and it drove him mad?"

"You might say that," the guy in the suit said.

Danny stood up next to C.D. and said, "I've seen that movie. It's not scary at all."

"Well, it seemed to convince Arthur," the guy in the suit said. He looked pleased when people laughed. "Anybody object if we run some of it tonight?"

"We already have a program for this evening," the fat guy in front said. "A six-month backlog of movie reviews."

The guy in the suit suggested they put it to a vote. The membership was divided about equally between those who wanted to see *The Hand of Irving* and those who wanted to hear the movie reviews. The guy in the suit suggested that those who wanted to hear reviews could go outside, and those who wanted to see the movie could stay. There was general agreement to that, and a number of old men went outside—though not as many as had voted for the reviews.

A couple of guys who were shaped like bowling pins set up a movie projector and began to string film through it. "You have no video tape?" Frankie said.

One of the two bowling pin guys made an impolite snort and said, "Video tape's for sissies. If it's not on film, it's not a movie."

Elisa patted Frankie's hand.

Soon the lights went off, and the projector began to chatter. The movie was splashed onto the front wall of the room, vastly out of focus. Loud music thundered as the image sharpened.

The Hand of Irving was the tender story of a butcher named Irving who had beautiful hands. When he died, the local mad scientist—in this case, a Dr. Karimazov—dug up Irving, cut off his hands, and tried to make them come alive in the hope they would become pets for his lonely daughter, Ismerelda. The right hand was just fine, learning to fetch and roll over, but the left went bad. Its first victim was Ismerelda. Dr. Karimazov went crazy looking for the left hand, and at one point murdered the right hand by mistake. At the end, Dr. Karimazov and the left hand tussled on a bridge over Reichenbach Falls in Switzerland, and both fell to their deaths. The body of the hand—if a hand can be said to *have* a body—was never found.

Danny had been curious to see the movie again, if only to find out if he still agreed with his earlier opinion. And he did. The pace of the story was ponderous, the acting was unbelievable, and the special effects were unconvincing. By the time Dr. Karimazov began his search for the left hand many of the old men had gone outside to hear the reviews, and of those who'd stayed, three were snoring.

When the lights came on, the three guys down in

front were still asleep. Mr. Keegan and Danny were still awake, as were the monster kids. The only other person still conscious was the guy in the suit who'd done so much talking during the meeting. He rubbed his hands together and said, "Ya know, they don't take the same care with movies now as they used to." He looked around and said, to Danny and the others, "A classic, huh?"

"Certainly an old black-and-white movie," Elisa said.

"I have the hand, you know," the man said proudly.

"What?"

"The hand of Irving. The one used in that last scene at Reichenbach Falls. It's part of my collection." He stood up and strolled over and handed a business card to Mr. Keegan. Mr. Keegan read it out loud: "J. Manley Forest, collector of movie memorabilia and publisher of *Marvelous Movie Monsters* magazine."

"It's autographed," Mr. Forest said.

"What?" said C.D.

"The hand. It's autographed by Lazlo Peroshki, the stuntman who was inside it during that last scene."

"You mean it's big enough to wear?" Danny said.

"Big enough for me and Lazlo to wear, anyway," Mr. Forest said.

"Just a minute," Danny said, and went into a huddle with his father and his friends. While Danny spoke, the monster kids broke in with encouraging remarks, but Mr. Keegan didn't say anything.

"OK, Dad?" Danny said.

"OK by me. You'd better ask Mr. Forest, though."

Danny turned to Mr. Forest and said, "How'd you like to help save Mother Scary?"

"From Arthur Debarber?"

"Well," said C.D., "yes."

"Well, ya know, I'm not much of a fighter."

"You get to wear the hand suit," Howie said.

That seemed to surprise Mr. Forest. His face grew determined as he said, "Arthur and I go way back. Someday he'll thank me for doing this."

They worked out a few details with Mr. Forest. Much later, after Danny got home, he called Zelda Bella and said, "Come over to the Stein mansion tomorrow afternoon. We're all going to practice a little magic."

Chapter Ten

The Hand of Irving

Before Zelda Bella got the hang of what Danny and the monster kids had in mind, she pulled frogs from hats, wound up balls of fire out of nothing, and changed one of the Mad Room games into chocolate. It was a game called Roman Legion, and nobody played it much, so they decided to leave it that way. They nibbled on the chocolate as they continued.

Zelda Bella made all the frogs disappear, and the fire had been magical so it hadn't actually burned anything. Zelda Bella had a problem *not* doing magic, but she tried, and after a while she learned to turn it on and off. Of course, not being witches, the kids already had the hang of not doing magic. Before the sun went down, Frankie pronounced everybody ready.

"I'll take care of things at the TV station," Zelda Bella said as she hugged them all and left.

Danny knew that on Saturday he'd be going to the TV station again. He pleaded with his parents to not let

Barbara come with him. "We're fighting evil here," Danny said. "I wouldn't want Barbara to get hurt."

Mrs. Keegan said, "If there's a chance of *you* getting hurt, I'm not so sure you should go either."

The bottom dropped out of Danny's world as he realized the magnitude of the error he'd made. Frantically he said, "But I'm a year older than her. And I'm a guy. Besides, I promised."

Mr. Keegan said, "They're Danny's friends, dear. Barbara will have to learn some time that she and Danny, and even she and Elisa, are not joined at the hip."

Mrs. Keegan pursed her lips and nodded. "I'll see if she wants to help me with those shelves some unnamed husband has been promising for six months to put together."

Mr. Keegan looked sheepish.

Mrs. Keegan said, "Be careful, Danny. I want you to come home in the same condition in which you left."

"No problem, Mom. It's just a TV show."

A few hours later, while Mr. Keegan was out swimming at the local pool and Mrs. Keegan was keeping Barbara busy with the prefab metal shelving, Danny took the bus to the TV station. The same guard was there. He had Danny's name on a list, and there was no trouble getting in. Danny ran to Stage 5.

The Mother Scary set was quiet, which was odd because so many people were there. On one side of the set Arthur Debarber and Stevie Brickwald stood together. They each wore a Monster Masher uniform, though Stevie's had less braid and no medals. Stevie had a camera, and he kept holding it up to look through the viewfinder.

Glaring at the two Monster Mashers from the other

side of the set were the twelve perky old women Danny and the others had met at Zelda Bella's apartment at Halloween Acres. The witches were dressed nicely, as if they were going to office jobs in Manhattan, but the looks on their faces made Danny nervous.

Danny walked to them and nodded. They nodded back.

Arthur Debarber called out to Danny, "I am delighted to see you've come out in support of the Monster Mashers."

Danny said, "I'm not exactly here in support."

"As an independent observer, then," Arthur Debarber said, and winked broadly.

"I'm not observing, either."

"You can't be with them," Arthur Debarber said, and pointed accusingly at the witches.

"I can," said Danny, "if I want to."

Arthur Debarber's face closed. "Very well," he said as if it were not well at all. He looked away from him as if Danny were something disgusting. Stevie made faces at him. Danny tried not to look.

When the two cameramen and the sound guy arrived they seemed surprised to see so large an audience, but they soon forgot their surroundings as they began to check their equipment. The woman came by and dropped dry ice into the cauldron, making the water bubble and smoke. Zelda Bella, looking worried under her Mother Scary makeup, toddled in with her broom and a big cardboard box. She spoke for a few minutes to her friends, then set the box behind the cauldron and waited.

Four more people came in the enormous sliding door. From their silhouettes Danny knew they were his monster friends. He also knew that the one wearing the cape wasn't C.D. and the one carrying the enormous bone wasn't Howie.

Danny went to join them and said, "You guys about ready?"

"You sound worried, Danny," Elisa said.

"Who me? Just because nobody knows exactly what Arthur Debarber has in mind? Just because an angry witch who has no experience with curses is probably more dangerous than an evil witch who knows what she is doing? Why should I be worried?"

"You're a corker," Howie said, and wrapped his vampire cape tightly around his body the way he'd seen C.D. do.

"Who are all these people?" a voice shouted from behind Danny. He turned around and saw Tom the director waving papers in the air. "And why is this nut back on my set? Security!"

Zelda Bella talked quietly to Tom. Tom shook his head. She talked to him again, waving her arms. He shook his head. Zelda Bella spoke again, then stopped and waited with her arms folded. Tom studied her for a moment and then called out, "'All right, everybody. Air in five minutes. First guest making an unrehearsed peep is out on his or her ear."

The same woman who threw the dry ice into the cauldron now pushed the big door closed. Bright lights came on. Howie and C.D. took up positions on either side of Mother Scary. The Mother Scary music began and the show was on.

While Mother Scary introduced her nephews, Howler, who was C.D., and Fang, who was Howie, Stevie snapped photo after photo. Arthur Debarber scribbled notes on a spiral-bound pad.

C.D. waved his bone in the air while he threw back

his head and made a high, thready sound that was supposed to be a frightening howl, and Howie strutted around sucking something out of a thermos bottle through a straw.

"Pick a card, any card," Mother Scary said to Fang.

Fang took a card from the fan of them Mother Scary held up, and looked at it.

Mother Scary put her hand to her forehead as if concentrating and said, "Seven of diamonds."

"Amazing," said Fang, and held the card up to the camera. It was the seven of diamonds.

"Of course. They're all seven of diamonds!" Mother Scary shrieked, and threw the remainder of the deck into the air.

"What is today's movie?" Howler said.

"Glad you asked," Mother Scary said, and lifted a tube in front of her face. She looked through it with both eyes. "Empty tube," she said. Chuckling to herself like a contented chicken, she began to pull colorful scarves out of the tube and drape them around Fang, more and more until you couldn't see Fang's face. The last scarf was white. She held it up to the camera. On it were the words *The Hand of Irving*.

Danny was watching Arthur Debarber. When he saw the title of the movie, Arthur Debarber stepped back and mopped his forehead with a handkerchief he took from a pocket.

A Wonky Wheats commercial came on the television, and Tom said, "OK, everybody. Relax."

Ida and Ruth walked over to where Danny was standing with Elisa and Frankie. Ida said, "You are doing a fine job so far."

"The big test will be soon," Elisa said.

After the Wonky Wheats commercial was one for

Snuggly Mutts. When that was over, *The Hand of Irving* began. Arthur Debarber stayed where he was. He didn't go anywhere near where he would be able to see the television.

Danny walked over to Arthur Debarber, who looked at him warily. Stevie snapped Danny's picture and said, "Don't trust this guy, sir."

Danny ignored Stevie and said, "You know, this *Hand of Irving* movie is more great evidence for the existence of monsters."

"Maybe," said Arthur Debarber, "but I refuse to pollute my mind with such stuff."

"You tell him, sir," Stevie said.

"You're missing out," Danny said, and walked away shaking his head.

"It's not going to work," he said to Elisa, Frankie, Ida, and Ruth. "He won't look at the movie."

Ida said, "Then we're doomed. He'll never see how tame that flick is. He'll ship us all out."

"Then it is time," Elisa said. She twirled her finger high above her head. Shortly there was movement out in the darkness beyond the Mother Scary set. Ida pointed and covered her hand with her mouth. Everybody looked in the direction Ida pointed. A hand the size of a man crawled into the light making a terrible snuffling sound.

"The hand of Irving!" Arthur Debarber cried. He sounded hysterical.

The hand crawled in Arthur Debarber's direction, making about the same headway as a land tortoise. Arthur Debarber turned and ran.

"Wait!" Danny cried. "Let us explain."

Arthur Debarber, heedless of where he ran as long as he ran away from the hand, ran toward the witches. They reached out to him and screamed, "It's not what you think!'' But Arthur Debarber recoiled and ran the other way.

Elisa said, "You go that way. We'll go this way." The witches ran in one direction. Danny and his monster friends ran in the other. They tried to catch Arthur Debarber between them. "I say," cried Howie.

"What's going on?" Stevie shouted as the monster kids ran past.

"Let's have some light," Tom cried, and seconds later the whole stage was as bright as if somebody had rolled open the door.

Arthur Debarber ran to the far end of the stage and turned, his eyes full of fear. Everybody in the place was bearing down on him. "Stay back!" he cried, and turned to climb a narrow ladder. He climbed higher and higher, up to a catwalk that seemed to be miles above the floor. He took two steps out onto the catwalk and froze, his arms gripping the single skinny railing.

"Come down," Howie called. "We won't hurt you."

"The hand!" Arthur Debarber cried. "The hand of Irving!"

"A guy in a suit," Danny called to him.

"No. No. I was twelve. I saw it."

The hand crawled up behind them, snuffling louder now.

"Come down," Zelda Bella called.

"I can't. I'm afraid I'll fall."

"Let's rescue him," Howie said, and ran forward.

Ida caught Howie by one arm and swung him around. She said, "You can't go up there. It's too high."

"I'm not afraid of heights," Howie said.

"It's too high," Ida said with more determination.

"Grown-up logic," Frankie whispered to Danny. "We

are afraid of heights so you cannot climb." Danny nodded philosophically.

But nobody had hold of the hand of Irving. It was on the ladder now, climbing, finger over finger.

"No," said Arthur Debarber, and shuffled farther out onto the catwalk.

The crowd on the stage floor concentrated on the spectacle above in silence. The hand reached the catwalk and began to move along it. Arthur Debarber shuffled a little farther, then suddenly a foot slipped and he was hanging by one hand from the spidery railing. "Erp!" he cried.

The hand reached around Arthur Debarber's waist with one gigantic finger and pulled him back onto the catwalk. Danny cheered. He noticed that everybody else was cheering, too. Arthur Debarber held the tip of one of the hand's fingers and let it lead him to the end of the catwalk. The hand went first, and slowly, painfully, Arthur Debarber followed the hand to the floor. Both of them collapsed onto the ground.

Everybody ran over to them. Danny and his monster friends helped J. Manley Forest get his head out of the hand suit while Mother Scary held Arthur Debarber's head in her lap.

"Drink some of this," Ruth said, and plunged the thermos Fang had been drinking from into Arthur Debarber's hands.

Arthur Debarber shied away and said, "Yech! Fluid of Life."

"Cherry soda," Howie said.

"Ah," Arthur Debarber said, and took a sip. He smiled and looked over at the head protruding from the hand suit.

"J. Manley Forest!" Arthur Debarber exclaimed.

"At your service, sir," Mr. Forest said, and tried to bow.

"I don't remember the hand of Irving snuffling like that."

"It didn't in the movie. But, ya know, there's a lot of dust in this suit now, and it didn't do anything good for my sinus condition."

Arthur Debarber looked up at Zelda Bella's face looking down into his. "Well, I seem to have been wrong about witches." He thought about that for a moment. "I started the Monster Mashers because *The Hand of Irving* scared me so much when I was twelve. I didn't want anybody else to have that terrible experience. But you know, if the movie is still on, I'd like to take another look at it. The hand saved my life. I owe it that at least."

"Come on," said Tom. "There's still plenty left."

As they walked back to the Mother Scary set, Danny caught Stevie's eye and winked. Stevie just looked confused and let down.

Tom set up a chair in front of the monitor, and Arthur Debarber sat in it. As he watched *The Hand of Irving* he made comments. He said "This isn't scary!" and "This is just boring. What a snoozer!" and "Fake! All fake!"

Then the movie was over and Mother Scary did her closing gags. Then the show was over, and somebody opened the big sliding door and the hot, bright lights above the set were turned off. Arthur Debarber said, "My entire life has been based on a misconception." He tore the braid from his shoulder. "Monster Mashers is no more."

Stevie Brickwald had been watching him with increasing alarm. Now he said, "Aren't we going to deport anybody?"

90

Arthur Debarber looked at him with mild surprise and said, "Why would we want to do that?"

"Hurray!" Danny and his friends shouted.

Stevie kicked Arthur Debarber in the shin and stomped off. He threw his hat on the floor as he walked, and then his jacket.

"Now, there goes a real monster," Danny said.

MEL GILDEN is the author of the acclaimed *The Return of Captain Conquer*, published by Houghton Mifflin in 1986. His second novel, *Harry Newberry Says His Mom Is a Superhero*, will be published soon by Henry Holt and Company. Prior to these novels, Gilden had short stories published in such places as *Twilight Zone—The Magazine*, *The Magazine of Fantasy and Science Fiction*, and many original and reprint anthologies. He is also the author of four previous hair-raising Avon Camelot adventures featuring Danny Keegan and his fifth grade monster friends, *M Is For Monster*, *Born To Howl*, *The Pet Of Frankenstein*, and *Z Is For Zombie*.

JOHN PIERARD is a freelance illustrator living in Manhattan. He is best known for his science fiction illustrations for *Isaac Asimov's Science Fiction Magazine*, *Distant Stars*, and SPI games such as Universe. He is co-illustrator of Time Machine #4: *Sail With Pirates* and Time Traveler #3: *The First Settlers*, and is illustrator of Time Machine #11: *Mission to World War II*, Time Machine #15: *Flame of the Inquisition*, and most recently *M Is For Monster*, *Born To Howl*, *There's A Batwing In My Lunchbox*, *The Pet of Frankenstein*, and *Z Is For Zombie*.